Published in Australia by
Books To Inspire Press
Perth, Western Australia
dianasmithbookstoinspire.com
author@dianasmithbookstoispire.com

First published in Australia in 2024
Text Copyright © Diana Smith 2024
Illustrations Copyright © Shay Fletcher

All rights reserved. No part of this publication may be reproduced, stored in a retrieval system, or transmitted, in any form or by any means without the prior written permission of the publisher, nor be otherwise circulated in any form of binding or cover other than that in which it is published and without a similar condition being imposed on the subsequent purchaser.

National Library of Australia Cataloguing in Publication entry

 A catalogue record for this book is available from the National Library of Australia

ISBN: 978-0-6456058-9-1 (paperback)
ISBN: 978-1-7635896-3-6 (hardcover)
ISBN: 978-1-7635896-2-9 (ebook)

Illustrations by Shay Fletcher
Edited by Brooke Anne Olive
Printed by Ingram Spark

Disclaimer: All care has been taken in the preparation of the information herein, but no responsibility can be accepted by the publisher or author for any damages resulting from the misinterpretation of this work. All contact details given in this book were current at the time of publication, but are subject to change.

Wild Walpole School Adventure

WRITTEN BY DIANA SMITH

ILLUSTRATIONS BY SHAY FLETCHER

Chapter 1

The day was cold. The day was grey. It was winter and raining.

Sam and Jess stood together next to the bus. It was time for the school camp.

Ben and Tim were not there. Ben and Tim were late. This was usual for Ben and Tim.

The boys rushed down the path, their bags swinging everywhere.

"Wait for us!" yelled Ben.

"We made it," laughed Tim.

The girls sighed. Sometimes Ben and Tim were more trouble than they were worth.

All the students began to pack their stuff on the bus.

They had tents, torches and sleeping bags. They had fishing rods, camp chairs and suitcases.

They needed lots of gear to camp in Walpole.

It would be cold. It would be exciting.

All the kids climbed on the bus, laughing and joking.

The holidays were over and school camp was just starting.

It didn't feel like school. It felt like an adventure.

All of the kids began to sing. All of the teachers began to frown.

Chapter 2

The bus travelled through the trees, winding along the country road.

Nature was all around. They saw cows and birds, sheep and kangaroos.

On the bus, Jess slept. Next to her Sam was texting Ben.

Ben and Tim were laughing and teasing the girls who sat in front.

Sam was mad. Ben should have been texting back.

She got up.

"Sit down Sam," said the teacher.

"Yes Miss," said Sam.

Ben looked up and saw Sam upset.

Ben checked his text.

Sam was mad.

Jess woke up and saw Sam's face.

"What happened? What did I miss?" she asked Sam.

"Jess, the boys were playing around with the girls in front."

"Who? Mel and Tia?" Jess asked.

"Yeah," Sam frowned.

"Don't worry. It's nothing. Those boys would annoy anyone."

Sam thought about that. Jess was right.

Ben and Tim loved to joke around. Maybe she was just being silly. Maybe she was jealous?

Sam got a text. It was from Ben. It read: Sorry. X Upside down smiley face.

Sam texted a smiley face back.

Ben looked at Sam. They smiled. It was fine.

Ben turned to look at Tim.

"Tim, we have to behave better sometimes. Phew, my girl almost murdered me."

Tim didn't reply. He had fallen asleep.

Chapter 3

The bus pulled into the campsite near Mount Frankland. All around were many tall trees.

Everyone got off the bus. It was cold and wet, but the air was fresh and clean.

"What are these trees called Miss?" asked a student.

"These trees are mostly Tingle, Jarrah and Karri trees. They are very famous for their height and beauty," replied Miss Metts.

Miss Metts was Sam's favourite teacher.

It was time to set up camp. The students had to put up their tents, unroll their sleeping bags and sort out their gear.

It took a long while and was harder than it looked.

"Maybe we should ask for help," said Tim.

Tim's side of the tent kept collapsing. Ben's side of the tent was missing a few poles.

"Nah, we'll be right," laughed Ben.

Ben had been camping before. In his backyard. With his

dad. He felt like an expert.

On the other side of the campsite, the girls were setting up their tent.

They followed the instructions.

Their tent was almost ready.

They even had a front doormat.

Soon they were sitting inside, warm and dry, eating snacks.

"We are going fishing soon. Then down the river in a kayak. I can hear the water from here!" Jess laughed excitedly.

"That's a river? I thought we were near a beach! I hope we don't have to touch the fish if we catch one," shuddered Sam. "They are so gross!"

Chapter 4

Soon all the students were outside.

They sat on logs. They listened to the instructions about fishing and kayaking.

Tim and Ben were on the other side of the group. Ben sat next to Tia. Tia was scared.

Tia did not like water. Tia did not like fishing.

"I don't want to go, Miss Metts," she said.

Ben looked at her. Tia looked worried.

"Tia, you will be fine, I promise. Ben will be your partner today. He is an expert when it comes to camping, right Ben?" asked Miss Metts.

Ben felt proud. Then Ben felt worried. He wasn't really an expert. He didn't know very much at all. But he could not back out now.

"Sure, no worries, Miss," he smiled.

Sam was upset. She wanted to be Jess' partner. She thought Tim would be Ben's partner.

Now somebody would be left out. And maybe Ben liked

Tia now? Sam was also angry at Miss Metts.

"Can we choose our own partners Miss Metts?" asked Jess.

"Yes, the rest of you may pair up and then we will split into two groups. Half of you will go with Mr Kerry for fishing. The other half of you will go kayaking. We'll all be meeting back here for dinner. Make sure you stick with your groups. I don't want anyone lost!"

Chapter 5

Jess and Sam were in Miss Mett's group. They put on lifejackets before climbing into their kayak.

"Jess?" said Sam.

"Yes Sam?" replied Jess.

"Aren't you worried about Tim maybe being partnered with another girl?" asked Sam.

"Is this about Ben and Tia going fishing together?"

"Of course!" exploded Sam. "It's totally unfair how she ends up near Ben all the time. And he doesn't even care or notice!"

Jess didn't know what to say. "Alright Sam," she replied.

The girls paddled in silence for a moment. The sun peeked through the clouds. On the shore, blue wrens flitted about the trees.

"Look Sam. Aren't those birds pretty?" said Jess. She pointed to the shoreline.

Sam sighed. Having a boyfriend was hard. Being worried about a boyfriend was hard. But she was missing out on having fun with her best friend. And Ben liked her. At least she hoped Ben liked her.

"Jess, do you think Ben likes me?" Sam asked.

"Yes, he likes you. But he is also friends with Tia's brother. He'll look out for her. I don't think he is an expert at camping though. Didn't he only camp in the backyard with his dad that one time?"

Sam laughed. Jess was right.

She didn't need to worry about this sort of stuff anymore.

The girls paddled on.

All around them, the other students laughed and splashed and pointed at the wildlife they could see.

Chapter 6

Back on the river's edge, Tim cast out his fishing line for the tenth time.

Tim was bored. Tim was cold. Tim was hungry.

"I'm bored. I'm cold. I'm hungry!" he whined.

"Quit whining Tim and catch our dinner!" said Ben.

Ben was struggling with Tia's fishing rod. She had made a mess of the line and it was knotted.

Being an expert was not easy! Looking after Tia was not easy either.

Ben played football with Tia's brother, Kade.

Kade was big and Kade was fast. Ben would make sure Tia was okay.

Tia and Mel sat together under the trees. They were chatting about the next school dance.

Mel wanted to go with Tia. Tia didn't want to go. Tia wanted to see her boyfriend, Mark.

Mark went to another school. He was very smart. Mark studied hard. Tia studied hard. They liked to study together.

"These boys are terrible," said Tia. "Ben's only pretending to be an expert. Look! He just stepped right into the water with his shoes on!"

"They are such goofs," said Mel. "I have no idea why Sam and Jess put up with them!"

"Did you see Sam's face when Miss Metts made me go with Ben? I think she was upset," worried Tia.

"Sam will be fine. It's Ben you have to worry about," laughed Mel.

"Why Ben?" questioned Tia.

"Cause he's definitely not the expert he claims to be!" giggled Mel pointing to the boys.

Ben and Tim were tangled in each other's fishing lines. Ben splashed backwards into the water and fell over. Tim dropped his fishing rod and it began to float away.

Nearby, Mr Kerry shook his head. Mr Kerry did not feel like he was paid enough to deal with students like Tim and Ben. Students like Tim and Ben made Mr Kerry want to retire early.

Chapter 7

A long way up the river, Jess and Sam were paddling together.

It was very calm and relaxing on the water.

All the other students and teachers had paddled far away out of sight.

The trees were so tall they felt like giants above them.

Jess leaned all the way back in the kayak.

"What are you doing you wally?!" asked Sam.

"I'm trying to see the treetops, but my neck doesn't go back that far!" laughed Jess.

"Yeah, I have never seen trees this big before ever. How tall do you think they are?"

"Depends on the tree. The Karri tree grows up to 90 metres, and the Tingles are massive too. They can get to around 70 metres and Jarrah trees are like their little cousins at about 50 metres."

"Jess! How do you know all that?" exclaimed Sam.

"I read the camp brochure. Didn't you?" asked Jess.

"No, but maybe I should have!" laughed Sam.

Together both the girls leaned back in the kayak, trying to see all the way to the treetops above them.

It was a bad idea.

The kayak suddenly rolled and the girls were in the river!

Chapter 8

Back at camp, Ben and Tim changed their clothes and sat with their group around the warm fire.

Two by two the kayakers arrived back at camp.

It was hard work pulling the kayaks up onto the shore. Ben helped Miss Metts drag hers up.

"Miss Metts where are Sam and Jess?" he asked.

"Sam and Jess? They aren't here yet?" she asked.

Miss Metts looked worried. Ben felt sick. Where was Sam? Was she okay?

The teachers stood at the edge of the water looking up and down the riverbanks, talking and pointing.

Tim sat down and put his head in his hands. He had spent the day whining about being cold and bored and hungry while Jess might be lost. Lost forever! He felt awful.

Ben was pacing back and forth. He was mad at himself. He should have sat next to Sam before they were put in groups. Then he could have been her partner. Maybe then she wouldn't be lost!

A few kilometres away, the girls made it to shore, shaking and shivering. They were so grateful to have worn their lifejackets.

"Jess, what will we do?" cried Sam. "We could be lost here forever! What about snakes? What about crocodiles!" Sam began to sob.

"Samantha! You better pull yourself together. First of all, there are no crocodiles here. And it's a little too cold for snakes," Jess said sternly.

"How do you know for sure though?" asked Sam.

"I read the silly brochure remember?" said Jess matter of factly. "Now stop crying and calm down. If we panic, we can't think straight. We need to be calm and figure out what to do if we are here overnight."

"Overnight? H to the N to the O, Jess. We cannot be here overnight. We'll freeze to death," exclaimed Sam.

"Okay let me think, we better get as dry as possible then. Do you have anything for a fire?" asked Jess.

"Do I look like I carry a lighter Jess?"

"Maybe? I don't know! We could try that dry stick thing where we rub it together?" said Jess hopefully.

"This is ridiculous. Maybe there is a path around here somewhere we could follow back to the camp?" said Sam.

Both girls turned and looked at the bush behind them. It seemed much too thick to walk through. And there wasn't much room on the shore. There were no footprints around.

The whole place was deserted. It was eerie and quiet.

"Maybe we could build a raft Sam? Or swim back downstream?" said Jess.

"None of those seem like good options Jess."

The girls huddled together shivering. Far off in the distance their kayak floated further and further away. The two oars were long gone also.

Chapter 9

Back at camp, Ben clipped on a life jacket. It was growing dark and the teachers had decided to send Miss Metts and Mr Kerry up the river to look for the girls.

Ben wanted to go too. He wasn't taking no for an answer. Mr Kerry was unsure. He thought Ben was too silly to be trusted on the water this late in the day.

"Please Mr Kerry, I promise I'll listen to you. Sam and Jess need all the help they can get," begged Ben.

"Alright, but do exactly what I say, when I say! We'll need another volunteer to help as well."

Tim stood up from the river's edge. He was holding an oar that had just floated down. It was from the girls' kayak.

"I'll come. I want to help too."

"Alright Tim, get sorted so we can go before it's too dark," huffed Mr Kerry.

Chapter 10

Jess and Sam sat together by the shore's edge. They were scared and cold. They were hungry.

Behind them, they had built a makeshift shelter. It was made of branches and leaves. It would keep the wind and rain out.

"We just have to wait until somebody comes looking," said Jess.

"And if they don't, we figure out a new plan in the morning."

"That's right Sam, it's not so bad. At least we are together! We could be stuck with one of the teachers!"

The girls laughed.

"Should we sing? Would that be too weird?" asked Sam.

"Nah, let's do it."

The girls began to sing. It wasn't so bad. It would be nicer to have a fire and some food and maybe not be so wet. But it wasn't as scary anymore. It was almost night. But they felt peaceful and calm.

Suddenly they heard something!

"Look Jess! Look!" Sam jumped up pointing.

Paddling furiously through the water were Miss Metts and Mr Kerry.

Behind them in another kayak were Ben and Tim, towing an empty kayak behind them.

"Over here! We are over here!"

The girls shouted and jumped up and down. They were easy to spot in their bright yellow lifejackets.

The rescuers arrived and pulled their kayaks onto the shore.

Ben ran and hugged Sam who burst into tears immediately.

Jess was calm, unlike Tim, who had also burst into tears. She patted his back and laughed.

"Well, that's a relief," said Miss Metts.

"There's always one rescue each excursion. I have to stop signing up for these things," laughed Mr Kerry.

"Thanks so much for saving us," Sam said.

"Thank Ben and Tim, they're the experts!" laughed Miss Metts.

ABOUT THE AUTHOR
DIANA SMITH

Diana Smith is an award winning children's author and presenter whose work focuses on emotional intelligence and the introduction of key life concepts like self-love, mental resilience and gratitude. Her books are warmly inclusive and encouraging to all levels of readers.

To view more of her work, visit
www.dianasmithbookstoinspire.com

ABOUT THE ILLUSTRATOR
SHAY FLETCHER

Shay is a self taught artist from Dunsborough WA, who likes drawing and the beach. He is inspired by the human form and capturing it in motion. He likes artists such as Kim Jung Gi and Karl Kopinski, and hopes to become like them someday.

To see more of his work, his Instagram is
@microwaveooohsya

www.ingramcontent.com/pod-product-compliance
Lightning Source LLC
LaVergne TN
LVHW090054080526
838200LV00082B/2